A Place for Elijah

For my husband, Michel Ruben.
In memory of his parents Herb and Charlotte. —K.E.R.

For Uncle Charlie, in his memory. —J.F.

KAR-BEN PUBLISHING
A division of Lerner Publishing Group, Inc.
241 First Avenue North
Minneapolis, MN 55401 USA
1-800-4-KARBEN

Website address: www.karben.com

Main body text set in BreweryCom 17/20.
Typeface provided by Linotype AG.

Library of Congress Cataloging-in-Publication Data

Ruben, Kelly Easton, author.
    A place for Elijah / by Kelly Easton Ruben ; illustrated by Joanne Friar.
        pages cm
    Summary: "A family celebrates Passover, making sure they lay an extra place setting for the prophet Elijah. But when their neighbors lose power and stop by to get out of the cold, Sarah is worried that there won't be a seat left for Elijah"—Provided by publisher.
    ISBN 978-1-4677-7841-1 (lb : alk. paper)
    ISBN 978-1-4677-7846-6 (pb : alk. paper)
    ISBN 978-1-4677-9611-8 (eb pdf)
    [1. Passover—Fiction. 2. Elijah (Biblical prophet)—Fiction.] I. Friar, Joanne H., illustrator. II. Title.
PZ7.E13155Pl 2016
[E]—dc23   2015016338

Manufactured in the United States of America
1 – CG – 12/31/15

A Place for Elijah

Kelly Easton Ruben

Illustrated by **Joanne Friar**

KAR-BEN
PUBLISHING
www.karben.com

It is the first evening of Passover.

Mama and Sarah set the table. "We mustn't forget to make a place for Elijah," Sarah says.

Every year at Passover, Sarah sets a place and leaves the door ajar so Elijah the Prophet can come in and visit the seder.

"I would never forget," Mama says, "but it's awfully cold to leave the door open."

Outside the window, a cold wind blows. Fat raindrops tap the pane: *Let us in.*

Papa brings the colorful Passover plate. Little Jacob brings in matzah wrapped snugly in a napkin. "I have a job too!"

Sarah counts the places at the table. There are six places, and five in their family: Mama, Papa, Ruthie, Jacob, and Sarah. That leaves an empty seat.

"Elijah will sit next to me," she says.

Mama lights a fire. The flames yell at the cold with hot tongues: *Go away!*

"So cold for spring," says Papa as he looks out the window.

Across the street are shops with apartments above, where the shop owners live: Music Man Miguel, Doughnut Dan, Bagel Ben, Mrs. Faaiz who arranges flowers—and the boy who sells magazines and chews bubble gum.

The sky is melting from blue to gray. Soon it will be dark. The lit up windows across the street go off and on.

"Look," Jacob says. "The eyes of the buildings are blinking. Now they're closed."

"The power has gone off on the other side of the street," Papa says.

"Oh no," Sarah says. "The neighbors will get cold."

"I hope it's fixed soon," Mama says. "Everyone, wash your hands."

The family begins their Passover seder. They say prayers, including one for power to return for the neighbors. They tell stories about Moses and the Jewish people escaping from slavery into the promised land.

"Did you hide the afikomen?" Jacob asks Papa.

Later, the youngest child will find the hidden piece of matzah and get a prize. That is Jacob.

Papa winks, which means yes.

Suddenly a hubbub on the stairs and a knock on the door.

"It's Elijah the prophet!" Jacob says.

"He doesn't knock. He just slips in," Ruthie tells him.

Mrs. Faaiz carries a bouquet of tulips from her shop. "I don't have any light," she says.

"Please join us for dinner," Mama tells her.

Mrs. Faaiz sits in Elijah's seat.

"I'd better set another place," Sarah says.

"Did I take someone's seat?" Mrs. Faaiz asks.

"No," Mama and Papa say at once.

Sarah sets a new place for Elijah. She pulls up another chair.

Now there are six people and seven seats, including the empty chair for Elijah.

Papa serves chicken soup, fragrant with dill and onions, a matzah ball floating like a tasty island in the broth.

He explains the Passover meal to Mrs. Faaiz. He tells her about the matzah, and how the Jewish people had to leave Egypt before their bread rose.

He tells her about the seder plate too. "There is an egg for life, horseradish for the bitterness of slavery in Egypt, parsley and salt water for tears, and a bone to remind us of the sacrifice they used to make in the Temple long ago..."

"And charoset!" says Jacob, pointing to the chopped apples with honey and nuts.

"Yes," laughs Papa. "On Passover, everything has a story, even food. The charoset reminds us of the mortar the slaves used for making bricks."

A scuttle on the stairs, and a knock on the door.

Bagel Ben comes in. "I was about to heat a can of soup when the power went out."

"No one wants cold soup," Papa says.

"We're so glad you came," Mama says.

Bagel Ben sits down in Elijah's new seat. Mama tells Sarah with her eyes not to say anything so that Bagel Ben will feel welcome.

Quietly, Sarah sets another place, so that there are seven people, and eight seats, including one for Elijah.

A minute later, Doughnut Dan stumbles in, tripping on Yettie the cat in the hall. "Yours is the only light on the street," he says.

Sarah adds another place, so there are eight people and nine seats squashed in.

Ruthie clears the soup bowls. Sarah serves gefilte fish nestled on curves of green lettuce, with a dollop of purple horseradish.

She makes sure the door is open, so Elijah can still slip in.

Papa tells the story of frogs and gnats and locusts plaguing Egypt. He drops ten drips of grape juice on his plate to show sympathy with the Egyptian people for every plague.

Then a ruckus and no knock, just a little monkey in a cap and vest, running circles around the table.

"Manny!" Music Man Miguel chases after the monkey. "You have to knock!"

"Come join us," Mama says.

"Manny was cold," Miguel explains.

The monkey jumps on his shoulder. He picks at the flowers pinned to Mrs. Faaiz's dress, pulling off petals.

Miguel sits in Elijah's chair, so Sarah pushes the chair from Papa's desk to the table.

There are nine people, and this is the only chair left in the house.

Sarah helps Mama carry in brisket, asparagus, red cabbage, and potatoes sprinkled with parsley. Ruthie sets down tzimmes rich with carrots and raisins. "Still dark across the street," she says.

"We've got plenty of blankets, if the power stays off," says Mama.

"A Passover slumber party!" cries little Jacob.

Then, a whoosh on the stairs, a tiny knock, then creak and crack, as the door opens.

Is it Elijah the Prophet?

"Your door was open." The boy who sells magazines stands shyly inside.

His face is covered in sticky pink gum. "It was dark, so I couldn't see my bubble and it popped all over my face."

"Oh dear," Mama says. She gets a wet cloth to wipe off the gum. "Come join us."

"There's plenty for everyone," Papa says.

The boy sits in the last seat in the house. He sets his bubble gum neatly on the corner of his plate, heaped with food by Ruthie.

Sarah's heart sinks. Ten people, ten chairs, and no place left for Elijah.

Will Elijah feel unwelcome, and not come at all?

Suddenly, Manny the monkey leaps onto the table, grabs a piece of matzah, and jumps back up onto Miguel's shoulder.

Manny bites down and crumbs rain down on Miguel's head.

Everyone laughs, even Sarah.

"Thank you," says the bubble gum boy. "This is the best food I've ever had in my life."

"I've bought magazines from you," Papa says. "But I don't know your name."

"It's Elijah," the boy says.

"Finally!" little Jacob shouts. "I knew you'd come! And Sarah did too."

Sarah smiles at the boy. You never know how Elijah comes, only that he does.